GOODNIGHT, GOODNIGHT

Eve Rice
GOODNIGHT, GOODNIGHT

264

OAK ST. FLOWERS

Florist

Greenwillow Books, NEW YORK

The black drawing is a multimedia combination of lithographic crayon, black pencil, and pen and ink; an overlay for the yellow was prepared on acetate.

Library of Congress Cataloging in Publication Data   Rice, Eve.   Goodnight, goodnight.
Summary: Goodnight comes to all the people in the town and to the little cat as well.
[1. Night—Fiction] I. Title.   PZ7.R3622Go   [E]   79-17253
ISBN 0-688-80254-0   ISBN 0-688-84254-2 lib. bdg.

For the Mattisons—
Sr., Jr., and Jr. Jr.

Goodnight came over
the rooftops slowly.

"Goodnight," said the man
in the window in the tower,

"Goodnight," said the
chestnut vendor down below,

and a lady coming home,

and a mama to her baby,

while one little cat on the
roof all alone said,

"Won't someone come
and play with me?"

creeping slowly with the dark.

"Goodnight," said a man to
his parrot on a perch,

and a lady on TV
to anyone at all,

and the fireman nodded
when the big policeman called,

"Goodnight, Harry."
"Goodnight."

"Goodnight," said the woman
sitting sipping tea

to the sleepy dog
curled up in a ball,

while up on the roof,
the little cat meowed so softly,

But Goodnight came here

and Goodnight went there,
all over town.

"Goodnight," said the girl
when her mother finished reading.

"Goodnight," said her mother
and her father and her brother.

Goodnight settled softly

on the buildings all around,

while up on the roof,
one little cat purred

to his mother who had found him,
"Goodnight, Mother Cat."

"Goodnight."